Amelia falls in love

Amelia falls in love

Laura James

Illustrations by Lucy Truman

RYLAND
PETERS
& SMALL

LONDON NEW YORK

For J, with love.

Designer *Sonya Nathoo*
Senior editor *Annabel Morgan*
Production *Gemma Moules*
Art Director *Gabriella Le Grazie*
Publishing Director *Alison Starling*

First published in the
United Kingdom in 2005 by
Ryland Peters & Small
20–21 Jockey's Fields
London WC1R 4BW
www.rylandpeters.com

Design and illustrations
© Ryland Peters & Small 2005
Text © Laura James 2005

10 9 8 7 6 5 4 3 2 1

ISBN-10: 1-84172-862-4
ISBN-13: 978-1-84172-862-9

Printed and bound in China

contents

Best-laid plans...

In which we meet the heroine of our story

Once upon a time, on the fairy-tale island of Arannstay, just north of Mull, lived the beautiful and slightly ethereal Amelia.

Gorgeous and enchanting, she was a cross between a young Audrey Hepburn and Bambi at his most vulnerable. Add to this a generous pinch of good-natured scattiness and a large helping of natural charm, and it is easy to see why Amelia proved irresistible to everyone she met.

All her life Amelia had lived on the island and she loved every last inch of it. She spent her days wandering the corridors of the tumbledown castle or walking through the fields playing with the adorable black and white lambs. Often she would simply sit on the shore, staring out towards the mainland, counting her lucky

stars that she lived somewhere so utterly charming. Apart from its inability to satisfy her constant craving for new shoes, Arannstay was Amelia's idea of heaven. The village shop sold an unusual array of goods, but the footwear department inexplicably only stocked one pair of purple, size nine, thigh-length waders.

Amelia's father – an eminent if slightly eccentric writer, who had become famous for his biography of an 18th-century Russian botanist – bought the island one June afternoon in 1978. It was the day after he had met Amelia's mother.

Love strikes in strange ways and, while many feel roses are a perfect token of affection, Amelia's father felt any gift smaller than an island would fail to convey the depth of his passion. Amelia's mother, a world-famous model, gave up her glamorous career and moved to the island.

From that day forward, she spent her time caring for Arranstay's population of depressed donkeys and nursing her husband's writer's block, which she did with unfailing good humour. The couple's happiness was sealed with the arrival of their beautiful daughter.

Years passed and each day Amelia became more delicious. Life on the island was simple, the family surviving on a diet of hugs, vintage *Vogue* and banana custard. But things were about to change dramatically…

Amelia's parents were planning a trip to South America, her father to search for the lost Du Dugoo tribe and her mother to bring a little happiness into the lives of Peru's donkeys. After much soul-searching, they had decided not to take Amelia with them.

While Amelia's mother was deeply sad at the idea of time away from her beloved daughter, she realised that city life would open Amelia's mind, and possibly her heart, to a world of adventures.

And so, one afternoon, they sat Amelia down, gave her a huge bowl of custard and told her of their plan. She would travel to London and take up a position as personal assistant to the acclaimed artist Sir Douglas McDougall. She would have a year in London and then, when her parents returned to Arranstay from Peru, Amelia could (if she so wished) come home…

The recipe for the sustaining banana custard had been in Amelia's family for generations. In fact, without it some wonder whether the family would have survived so long. Once, many years ago, there was a shortage of eggs on the island. Not too big a problem, one might think. But, alas, the eggs were very special indeed, produced only by a rare breed of chicken.

Without his daily custard fix, Amelia's father found it impossible to work. Paralysed by writer's block, he was like a bear with a sore head. Amelia's mother tried to find some other dish to cheer him up, but it was no good.

In the end – after much searching – she managed to track down eggs from similar chickens in Paris, and each Monday morning a delivery made its way to the island. Amelia's father's malaise lifted and life became normal again. Soon, he was even singing in the bath. The island chickens recovered and custard was soon back on the menu…

Amelia's Banana Custard

Ingredients

(Serves 4)

3 bananas

6 egg yolks

40g caster sugar

250ml single cream

250ml full-fat milk

Wrap the bananas in foil and place them in a pre-heated oven at 160˚C (325˚F)/gas 3 for 20 minutes.

In a heatproof bowl, whisk together the egg yolks and sugar. Pour the cream and milk into a large saucepan and heat until almost, but not quite, boiling.

Take the pan off the heat and slowly whisk the milk and cream mixture into the egg mixture a little at a time.

Take a heavy-bottomed pan and pour in the custard. Heat gently, stirring constantly for about 10 minutes. When the custard has thickened, pass it through a sieve into a bowl.

Chop the baked bananas into the custard and enjoy!

Follow Amelia's tips and find your own style...

Don't slavishly follow fashion. Instead, invest in a selection of carefully chosen wardrobe staples. These should include:

✳ Black cashmere sweater. Well looked after, it will last for years.

✳ Crisp white cotton shirt. Perfect dressed down with jeans or up with a stylish skirt.

✳ Good pair of jeans that fit perfectly. It makes sense to buy the best you can afford.

✳ Leather belt. Accessories make an outfit, and if chosen well will add instant gloss to anything.

✳ Black court shoes. There are so few things they won't go with.

✳ Go-anywhere loafers. JP Tod's have a fabulous collection.

✳ Killer shoes. To make you feel like a Hollywood star.

✳ Versatile jacket. One that's great with jeans for day, but also works as a smart cover-up on chilly evenings.

✳ Little black dress. A cliché, but it really can take you anywhere.

✳ Emergency glamour dress. The one ready for any occasion.

✳ Two bags. One for evening and one large enough for daytime.

✳ Fabulous lingerie. It doesn't matter if no one sees it; you will know you are wearing it.

✳ Signature scent. Something timeless, so you can wear it from your 18th to your 80th birthday.

Enchanted journey

In which Amelia takes the train to London

Amelia began her journey with a heavy heart – leaving Arranstay had been desperately difficult for her. As she sat in the waiting room at the station on the mainland, however, she found herself being temporarily distracted.

Occasionally shooting her a furtive glance, the most adorable man in the world was sitting opposite. Amelia felt startled; Arranstay offered many wonderful things, but did not normally stretch to delicious men. This was a feeling Amelia was quite unused to.

He was divine. Sea-green eyes sat under the sort of quizzical eyebrows that could only belong to someone both charming and intelligent. His nose was perfect and his mouth was designed for kissing. He seemed about to speak to Amelia when a voice came over the PA system and announced that the London train was ready for boarding. Amelia bent down to gather her belongings and, by the time she looked up, the man had disappeared.

Amelia sighed as she settled into her seat. Not long into the journey, she unpacked a picnic, spread a linen napkin on her lap and began to eat. Almost immediately she became aware of something wet and insistent nudging her knee.

Looking down, she saw a handsome if slightly scruffy Jack Russell. It was love at first sight. Amelia fed the dog a piece of pâté and stared into his huge plaintive eyes. He looked so lonely, she immediately felt they were kindred spirits. How the dog had ended up on the train, she did not know. But judging by his hunger and unkempt appearance he was a stray. Her heart filled with love and she desperately wanted to keep him.

A guard arrived and tried to take the dog away. But he began howling and upsetting the other passengers. The terrible noise stopped only when he was allowed to curl up at Amelia's feet (the dog, that is, not the guard).

With eight hours on the train looming before them, Amelia and the dog she had christened Jim curled up for a nap. Amelia slept fitfully, dreaming of the man she had seen in the waiting room. The dog slept deeply, dreaming of pâté and walks in the park.

When the train arrived, Amelia and Jim walked off into a world of noise and chaos so different from Arranstay, and began their new life in London…

Smoothest Chicken Liver Pâté

Trim the chicken livers. Melt 90g of the butter in a non-stick frying pan. Lightly sauté the chicken livers in the butter – this should take only a few minutes. Lift out the livers and set them to one side.

Add the onion to the pan and cook for 5–10 minutes until it is softened. Tip the livers, onion and butter from the pan into a food processor. Add a good grind of salt and black pepper, the cream and the rest of the softened butter, and blitz until the mixture is smooth.

Put the brandy in a pan and bring to the boil. Add it to the mixture in the food processor and continue to blitz. Push the pâté through a sieve into a terrine or ramekins, and place in the fridge for a few hours until it has set.

Ingredients

(Serves 4)

400g chicken livers

200g softened butter

1 onion, finely chopped

Salt and freshly ground black pepper

50ml double cream

Brandy

Standard White Loaf

Ingredients

650g strong white
 bread flour

1 tsp salt

Half a tsp sugar

1 sachet of instant
 dried yeast

Good splash of
 olive oil

400ml warm water

Mix together the flour, salt, sugar and yeast. Make a well in the centre of the dry ingredients, pour in the water and olive oil, and gradually combine the flour into the liquid until a dough is formed. Turn out on to a lightly floured surface and knead for about 10 minutes.

Put the dough back into the bowl and cover it with a clean tea towel. It needs to go somewhere warm to rise – an airing cupboard is perfect. Leave the dough for about an hour, or until it has doubled in size. Then take it out of the bowl and pound it until it deflates (this is enormous fun if you have had a difficult day, as it certainly eases frustration). Shape the dough into a loaf and place in a 1kg loaf tin or on a baking tray.

Put the dough back in the warm place and leave for another 30 minutes to rise. Put the tin or tray into an oven pre-heated to 220°C (425°F)/gas 7 and bake for about 35 minutes or until the bread is golden and sounds hollow when tapped on the base.

Chocolate Cake

Pre-heat the oven to 180˚C (350˚F)/gas 4.

Ingredients

(Makes about 8 slices)

250g softened butter

250g caster sugar

4 eggs

1 tsp vanilla extract

3 tbsp good-quality unsweetened cocoa powder

250g self-raising flour

4 tbsp full-fat milk

30g good-quality milk chocolate

30g good-quality dark chocolate

30g good-quality white chocolate

Beat together the butter and sugar until light and creamy. Break the eggs into a bowl, add the vanilla extract, and mix. Gradually beat the eggs into the butter and sugar mixture. Sift the cocoa powder and flour onto the mixture, add the milk and, using a metal spoon, gently fold in until fully blended. Smash the chocolate into small pieces and add to the cake mixture. Alternatively, throw everything into a food processor and whizz for a few minutes.

Pour the cake mixture into a greased 20 x 4 cm round cake tin. Bake for 30–40 minutes or until the cake springs back when gently pressed in the centre and has shrunk away from the sides of the tin. Turn the cake out onto a wire rack and let it cool.

Amelia won't leave home without...

Here are our heroine's tips on travelling in style:

✳ Take a soft blanket (cashmere, if possible). If it is chilly you can snuggle beneath it, or use it as a pillow if you wish to take a nap.

✳ Take a book that's truly diverting. Amelia usually travels with Stella Gibbons' *Cold Comfort Farm* or, if she is feeling nervous, a book from Enid Blyton's *Malory Towers* series.

✳ Wear something sensible but uplifting. There is little point in boarding a train in an organza confection. Equally, if you opt for something comfortable but hideous, you will arrive feeling deeply depressed.

✳ Shoes are important. The best for long journeys are Italian driving shoes – comfort with a hint of movie glamour.

✳ Take a notebook. Inspiration often strikes on a journey, so it is good to be able to jot down any interesting thoughts.

✳ Unless you're going to a fabulous hotel, take some essential luxuries. Amelia takes a scented candle, a bar of seriously luxurious chocolate and an audio book for when sleep is elusive.

✳ Music on demand. Whether you choose to pack an iPod or a battered Walkman, it is essential to ensure you have some fabulous music to listen to.

✳ Food for thought. Pack a gorgeous and indulgent lunch to help break up the journey and lift your spirits.

✳ A foreign-language edition of *Vogue*. It's such fun trying to work out what the words mean, but the pictures speak for themselves.

At home with Amelia

In which she finally meets her dream house

Amelia let out a sigh of pure contentment as she stood in the hallway of her new house. With Jim by her side she felt ready to begin a new chapter in her life. The house was tiny but gorgeous – like a doll's house, in fact. Situated in a mews, outside it was painted pink with pretty sash windows and a white front door with a brass knocker.

Inside was just as heavenly, but needed some attention. The kitchen was small and a little tired, so Amelia donned her rubber gloves and got stuck in. When every surface was gleaming, she moved into the sitting room and set about beating rugs and vacuuming the carpet. Once happy everything was perfectly clean, she set out to buy some essentials.

Amelia's first stop was an antiques market, where she bought linen sheets and a tea set covered in a riot of roses. Next she went to the ironmonger's for an old-fashioned bread bin, cake tin, tea and sugar tins and a hanging maid – just the thing for the old copper pans her mother had sent ahead for her. Her next stop was a department store, where she bought a Roberts radio in pastel blue and a pink checked tablecloth for the kitchen.

Later, sitting in a café sipping a milky latte, Amelia turned her attentions to her bedroom. Her room on Arranstay was still decorated as it had been when she was a child. But now she wanted a room that was pretty and sophisticated. 'My own boudoir,' she thought to herself with a giggle.

Scribbling a list in her notebook, she felt deliciously grown-up and, with Jim by her side, went in search of a fabric shop. A couple of streets away she found one and was soon looking delightedly at rolls of beautiful material.

Amelia arrived home tired but happy. Soon she was ripping open packages and finding a home for everything. After much hard work on Amelia's part, and a lot of tail-wagging on Jim's, the house was looking delicious.

'We deserve a treat after slaving away all day,' Amelia said to Jim, clipping his smart new lead to his collar. The pair set off for the park. Quickly discovering that Jim's favourite game was fetching a stick, Amelia found one he liked and threw it with force. Jim bounded after it excitedly, turning to make sure his mistress was still watching him.

Just as he was about to reach it, a stately deerhound arrived on the scene and picked up the stick as if it had always been hers. The two dogs stood facing each other and Amelia, feeling a little worried, briskly walked over. She reached them at exactly the same time as the other dog's owner.

'Grace,' he called, smiling apologetically at Amelia, who was rooted to the spot and unable to speak. It was the man from the railway station waiting room and he still appeared to Amelia to be heartbreakingly gorgeous. 'Oh help,' she thought as her heart began to beat at an alarming rate. Tall and broad-shouldered, with hair that flopped charmingly over one eye, Amelia had seen him in her dreams, but was surprised to have him standing in front of her. 'I'm Archie,' he said, smiling. 'And this is Grace.' 'I'm Amelia,' she stuttered as she gazed into his eyes. 'And this is Jim.'

Amelia's tips for a beautiful home

✳ Do not think you have to spend a fortune. Antiques markets, junk shops and charity shops are brilliant places to hunt out bargains or unusual pieces.

✳ Again, do not try to make your home fashionable. Instead, opt for an eclectic look and pick only those things that are beautiful, useful or both.

✳ Choose a couple of key colours for a room – greens and pinks work well together, as do browns and creams.

✳ Display cookware in the kitchen rather than hiding it in cupboards. It'll be easier to find and will make the room feel cosier.

✳ If you are renting or not planning to stay long in your home, invest in things you can take with you rather than spending a lot on paint or fitted carpets.

✳ Rugs, cushions and pictures all add an instant homely feel.

✳ Cheap glass jars make good storage containers for cotton wool and other bathroom essentials.

✳ Collages of your favourite snapshots in clear glass frames make a hallway or any other dead space feel more personal.

✳ If there is enough room, it is nice to have a desk in the bedroom; it can double as a dressing table, and is a good place to write letters.

* If you are lucky enough to have a real fire, burn scented wood to give your house a delicious scent.

* You cannot have too many candles. They're perfect for long, luxurious de-stressing baths and romantic dinners.

* A beautifully patterned tablecloth somehow adds instant warmth to any room.

Falling in love

In which Amelia loses her heart and finds her twin flame

Looking at Archie Amelia was instantly lost. He was, without a doubt, quite the most adorable man she had ever seen. He seemed to have been struck by the same bolt of lightening, and was gazing at her as if he had been trying to find her his whole life. He took Amelia's hand and, with their dogs trotting at their heels, they left the park to find a quiet café.

Jim and Grace lay under the table as Archie and Amelia drank creamy hot chocolate and exchanged life stories. Amelia was amazed to learn that Archie had grown up on a similarly deserted island. His father, Archie explained, was a notoriously reclusive trumpet player who came out of retirement only once a year to play at the Queen's birthday party and then promptly hotfooted it back to his island. Archie had been sent to London to see a bit of the world before going back to run the family farm. He was, he confessed to Amelia, missing the beautiful scenery, however, and until now his only consolation had been his doting deerhound.

Before long, Amelia and Archie became absolutely inseparable, spending much of their time walking the dogs, listening to old records and cooking delicious dinners for each other. Each night, when Amelia turned out the light, her very last thought was of

Archie. And each morning, when she woke, she rushed to ring him, so his would be the first voice she would hear.

Months passed and each day they fell deeper in love. They even adored each other's faults. Archie found it terribly sweet that Amelia had no sense of direction; she found it deeply endearing that he was always late. The dogs, too, missed each other and pined when they were separated.

All in all, London life was working out perfectly and, after a sticky start, Amelia loved her new job. Her first day had been a bit of a trial. Having boarded a bus going the wrong way up the King's Road, it felt like the end of the world when she ended up at World's End rather than Sloane Square.

Amelia was two hours late when, with Jim faithfully at her side, she arrived on Sir Douglas McDougall's doorstep. Gingerly, she knocked on the door. 'Whaddyawant?' he shouted as he opened the door. 'I, er, well the thing is…' Amelia tripped over her words as she struggled to say something sensible. 'Are you simple or something?' the man asked, now practically purple with rage. It was all too much for Amelia, who had only ever been treated with the utmost kindness, and she promptly burst into tears.

Suddenly realising that Amelia was both very young and very pretty, Sir Douglas' heart softened. 'Hush now,' he said, ushering her inside and handing her a large tartan handkerchief. 'You mustna mind me. Bark's much worse than me bite.' Amelia's smile lit up her face and from that moment the two of them became firm friends. Her job was interesting and diverting, but it did not stop her missing Archie terribly.

On their twelve-week anniversary, Amelia decided to cook Archie a surprise supper. Sir Douglas had kindly given her the afternoon off, and she spent it shopping at the local farmers' market.

By the time Archie arrived, the champagne was chilling in the

fridge, the candles were blazing, Amelia was radiant in a beautiful dress of rose-pink silk and there were delicious smells wafting gently from the direction of the kitchen.

Amelia was beside herself with excitement. Archie had been forced to make a trip back home, so she had not seen him for a whole week. Each day had felt like an eternity and, as there were no telephones on the island, they had not even spoken.

Used to the silence of Arranstay, Amelia had been surprised at how much she had missed her daily conversations with Archie. Although they had known each other for only three months, she almost could not remember life without him. They never ran out of things to say and, like many couples, seemed almost to have created their own language of in-jokes and reminiscences.

One of their favourite topics had been how they had met and how their beloved dogs had brought them together. In Archie, Amelia believed she had found her twin flame.

But now, one look at his face told her that something was very wrong indeed. Taking her hand, he led her to the sofa. There was, he said, something he had to tell her.

Fab Fish Pie

Pre-heat the oven to 170˚C (325˚F)/gas 3.

Ingredients

(Serves 2)

4 skinless and
  boneless salmon
  fillets

3 baby leeks,
  finely sliced

5 large potatoes,
  sliced

Salt and freshly
  ground black
  pepper

150ml double cream

Cover the bottom of an ovenproof dish with the salmon fillets and the leeks, arranging them evenly and fitting them in snugly so there are no gaps. Cover the salmon and leeks with the sliced potatoes. Sprinkle the pie with the salt and pepper, and pour over the double cream.

Place the pie in the oven for 1 hour 20 minutes. If the potato topping begins to brown too quickly, loosely cover the dish with aluminium foil.

Serve the pie with a green salad and freshly baked bread.

Soundtrack for a relationship

If music is the food of love, then one should ensure a balanced and delicious diet. Here are some of Amelia's top tunes to fall in love to, or to help console you if it all goes wrong:

When it's going well and you're walking on air...

✳ Van Morrison *Moondance* – hugely romantic and perfect when getting ready for a date.
✳ Aretha Franklin *I Say a Little Prayer* – for that 'I can't live without you' feeling.
✳ Georgie Fame *Sunny* – delivers that blissful 'I've finally found you' mood.

✳ Roxy Music *More Than This* – love at its most glamorous.
✳ Chet Baker *My Funny Valentine* – for when you are feeling at your soppiest.
✳ Ray Charles and Betty Carter *People Will Say We're in Love* – for when the relationship is still a delicious secret.
✳ The Waterboys *The Whole of the Moon* – because you're in love and it's cool.
✳ Louis Armstrong *What a Wonderful World* – surely the ultimate love song.
✳ Glen Campbell *Wichita Lineman* – perfect for those times when you can't be with each other.

When it's all going badly and all you want to do is lie on your bed and sob...

* Bill Withers *Ain't No Sunshine* – pure audio heartbreak.

* Nina Simone *Wild is the Wind* – for those utterly desperate moments.

* Dinah Washington *Drinking Again* – to remind you never to drink and dial.

* Ray Charles *Sittin' on Top of the World* – makes you realise that one day you'll get over it.

* Donny Hathaway *Jealous Guy* – for when you are eaten up by the green-eyed monster.

* Wasis Diop *Everything is Never Quite Enough* – for when you have done your best, but things have still gone horribly wrong.

* David Bowie *Letter to Hermione* – just to prove that boys cry too.

* Al Green *How Can You Mend A Broken Heart?* – absolutely perfect for all those painful 4am sobbing sessions.

* The Cardigans *Couldn't Care Less* – the ideal epitaph for a love that's died.

* Ray Charles *I Wonder Who's Kissing Her Now* – when the idea of him with somebody else is absolute torture.

* Jamie O'Neil *All By Myself* – for when you just have to sing and sob.

* Frank Sinatra *One More for My Baby* – for when those late-night regrets take hold.

Archie's secret

In which skeletons come out of the cupboard

Archie looked dreadful. 'Whatever's the matter, darling?' Amelia took his hand and looked up at him. Archie, almost in tears, kept apologising over and again and finally managed to blurt out his story. He had gone home, he said, to talk to his father and to try to find a way out of the awful mess he was in. Archie's mother had died when he was a small child and her last wish had been that Archie would marry Penelope, the daughter of her greatest friend.

It had been set in stone from that very time that the pair would marry when Penelope was 21. Her birthday was in six months and the families wanted to start planning the wedding. Archie had gone back to the island to break off the engagement, but his father would hear nothing of it. He had told Archie to go back to London and to get this new girl out of his system.

Amelia was devastated. Archie had lied to her. That he had done so to save her feelings did not make her feel any better. She asked him to leave. Truthfulness was important to Amelia and Archie's lies shook her to her very core. If he had lied about that, then what else might he have lied about, Amelia wondered. Perhaps he had never loved her at all. It was more than she could bear.

Amelia was beside herself with grief. She had fallen passionately in love with Archie and could not have imagined a life without him. Too distraught to eat or sleep, she was listless and cried endlessly. Sir Douglas was terribly worried and tried to coax her to eat by cooking vast pots of chicken soup and deliciously light cakes. Amelia tried to please him, but found that since Archie had gone nothing tasted the same.

Jim tried to cheer her up by nudging her knee with his nose, but even that did no good. Amelia distractedly patted his head, but all she really wanted to do was listen to sad songs and lie on her bed sobbing. Life without Archie had lost all its gloss. Each day she wished she could turn back the clock to when she was happy.

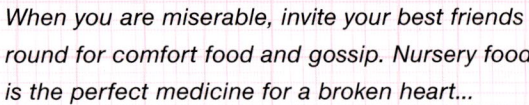

Creamy, Comforting Risotto

When you are miserable, invite your best friends round for comfort food and gossip. Nursery food is the perfect medicine for a broken heart...

Ingredients

(Serves 4)

40g butter

1 medium onion, chopped

320g arborio rice

1 glass white wine

1 litre hot chicken stock

Handful freshly grated Parmesan cheese

Chopped fresh herbs, such as basil and chives

Salt and freshly ground black pepper

Melt the butter in a heavy-based saucepan and sauté the onion until soft and translucent. Add the rice and stir until it is covered in the butter and has become transparent.

Add the wine and stir until it is absorbed. Add a ladleful of the hot stock and simmer. As the stock is absorbed, add another ladleful. Continue for about 20 minutes until the rice is creamy but still firm to the bite.

Stir in the Parmesan, herbs and seasoning, cover, and leave to stand for a couple of minutes.

Serve with a green salad and crusty bread.

First aid for a broken heart

In the early days of heartbreak, you need to look after yourself with the same care you would lavish on an abandoned puppy. Here are Amelia's tips for taking good care of yourself:

✳ Create a playlist of your favourite sad songs, but limit yourself to a couple of weeks of indulgent listening.

✳ Invite your friends round, open a bottle of wine, put on some soppy movies and break open a box of tissues. *High Society* and *Breakfast at Tiffany's* are perfect.

✳ Wear soft fluffy things that make you feel enveloped in a hug.

✳ Do not rush into a rebound relationship. Do all the girly things you never got round to when you were in a relationship.

✳ Buy a small plant and lavish attention on it. As it flourishes, your heart should slowly start to mend as well.

✳ Resist the temptation to call him. As each day goes by, your resolve will grow stronger and it will become easier.

✳ Schedule a month of treats. They do not need to be extravagant – just simple things like buying a new book or eating a whole box of chocolates. The idea is to make sure that there is something to look forward to every day.

Saying sorry

In which Amelia and Archie find each other... again

One morning, about three months after Archie had left, Amelia took Jim to the park. After a few minutes, she found herself walking past the spot where she and Archie had met. Strong until that point, she was horrified to find herself crying. She had tried hard to pull herself together, but everything reminded her of him.

He had left a sweater at her house and Amelia often snuggled up in it. She knew she ought to throw it out, but somehow she just could not. She played their song over and over again and, although she managed to give the appearance that she was coping, her heart had not mended and she doubted it ever would.

Suddenly, Jim raced off. Lately he had stayed at his mistress' side, almost as if he knew she needed to be treated with extra care. But something had caught his attention, and he was gone in a flash.

When ten minutes had passed and Jim had still not come back, Amelia started to worry. She walked their usual route, calling his name. Feeling a rising sense of panic, she asked some passers-by if they had seen him. No one had, and Amelia began to cry. Losing Archie was traumatic enough, but if she were to lose Jim as well, she simply would not be able to bear it.

After three hours of fruitless searching, Amelia set off for home. Jim, it seemed, had disappeared into thin air.

As Amelia turned the corner into the mews, her heart leapt. There he was on the doorstep. He was curled up, tail wagging, with Grace beside him and Archie keeping careful watch…

Archie started to walk towards her. His face was completely expressionless; she had no idea what he was thinking. Jim, having no such reserve, bounded over and, almost knocking her over, let out a bark of pure pleasure. By now she was crying. Were they tears of pain or joy? She thought she would never see Archie again and yet here he was – in her street, outside her house and with her dog. Amelia allowed herself to think how much he seemed to belong there.

'Amelia,' Archie said, taking her in his arms. 'I'm so sorry. I made a horrible mistake. I went home and got stuck into all the planning, but all I could think of was you. Last night, I couldn't take any more and went to see my father. When he realised how much I love you, he agreed it would be wrong for me to marry Penelope.'

Hours later – once Jim had been given a large bowl of chicken – Archie and Amelia sat at the kitchen table drinking coffee. Archie took Amelia's hand. 'Can you ever forgive me?' he asked, explaining that he had adored his mother. Her death had been so devastating that Archie had convinced himself he was doing the right thing in agreeing to marry his mother's choice of bride.

In the end, though, it had been his father who had put him right. They had talked late into the night about matters of the heart, and his father had told Archie how much in love with Archie's mother he had been when they married. Archie had understood every word, because that is exactly how he felt about Amelia.

Once Archie started talking about Amelia he had found it impossible to stop, and his father very soon had come to see that this was not some passing fancy, but true love. Amelia listened as Archie talked openly about how deeply he felt about her.

Archie's father had been sure that if Amelia was even half the girl that Archie had described, then his late wife would have thoroughly approved of the match. It brought a tear to his eye to see his son so grown-up and so obviously in love.

Lemon and Rosemary Chicken

Ask your butcher to spatchcock the chicken for you.

Ingredients

(Serves 2)

1 spatchcocked
  chicken

2 sprigs of fresh
  rosemary

Juice of 1 lemon

1 clove of garlic

Olive oil

Sea salt

Put the chicken in a zip-lock food bag. Pull the leaves off the rosemary and drop into the bag on top of the chicken. Squeeze in the lemon juice. Chop the garlic and add to the bag. Pour in the olive oil, zip up the bag and swish it around a bit. Pop the bag in the fridge and leave to marinate overnight.

Pre-heat the oven to 220˚C (425˚F)/gas 7. Take the chicken out of the fridge and allow it to reach room temperature. Place it in a roasting tin lined with foil and cook for about 45 minutes or until done (the skin should be crisp and the juices should run clear when the chicken is pierced with a sharp knife at the thickest part).

Cut the chicken into four pieces, arrange them on a plate and sprinkle over some sea salt. Serve with salad and devilled potatoes or rice.

Helping love endure

Getting back together can be hugely exciting, but also difficult. Here are Amelia's pointers to ensure the course of true love runs smoothly:

✳ Do not destroy the relationship with doubts. Talk honestly about your worries, and then leave it. When you are unsure, it is easy to nag, but few relationships can survive relentless scrutiny.

✳ Resist the urge to shout your reconciliation from the rooftops. Give yourself a few weeks to settle back into being a couple.

✳ Spend some time apart doing your own thing. It will make seeing each other more special. And just because you are back together,

do not drop your friends. After all, they were there for you when it all went wrong.

✳ Remind each other what it is that makes you want to be together. The most loving thing you can give one another is reassurance and support.

✳ Do not fall into the trap of trying to make everything wildly romantic. True love is about more than this, and it is the everyday that makes a relationship special.

✳ Look after each other. You probably said and did things when you were splitting up that are difficult to get over, and now is the time to nurture each other and your relationship.

Back together...

In which Amelia finds lasting happiness
and our story concludes

Eventually, after so much talking, Amelia began to feel sleepy. Archie and Grace left and she and Jim turned in. Her mind was whirring. Archie wanted her back, but could she trust him when he said he would not leave again? She felt so unsure about everything.

She fell asleep and dreamed of Arranstay. Life on the island had been so simple. She saw the lambs on the hillside and the mists rolling in over the sea with distant pipes providing the soundtrack. She missed her parents, and in her fitful sleep they were back together again, tucking into banana custard in the kitchen.

Amelia woke to the sound of her alarm. She called Sir Douglas and explained what had happened. As an artist, he was all too familiar with grand passions; he was understanding and told Amelia that she should follow her heart.

Amelia took Jim for a walk. Worried that he would run off again, she kept him firmly at heel. Unused to Amelia being so strict, Jim kept rolling his eyes at her and tugging at the lead. Patting him on the head but not relenting, Amelia walked briskly through the gates of the park and headed for the rose garden. Enjoying the heady scent of the flowers, she thought back to the night before. Archie had seemed sincere and genuine and he had looked awful, as if he had been pining as much for her as she had for him.

But what if it went wrong? She did not think she could go through all that pain again. On the other hand, surely it was worth taking a chance on a love this deep. 'We fit perfectly,' Amelia thought. 'Archie truly does feel like my other half.' And remembering how eaten up with jealousy she was when she had imagined him with Penelope only confirmed how deep her feelings ran.

When Amelia arrived home Archie was waiting for her. Clearly exhausted, as if he had not slept all night, he looked pleadingly at her. She invited him in and they sat on the sofa facing each other. The pain in his eyes was evident and Amelia felt a rush of love.

Archie took her hand and turned to face her. He opened his mouth to speak but she stopped him. 'I love you, Archie,' she said, leaning to kiss him. 'Oh Amelia,' he sighed, seeming as if he might cry at any moment. The dogs – clearly believing they were missing out on something – chose that moment to leap on to the sofa and cover Amelia and Archie in slobbering kisses.

'Well, they clearly approve!' Archie said, taking Amelia into his arms and vowing that he would never let her go again. Amelia sighed and snuggled closer to him. Sir Douglas had been right – when it had come down to it, she knew she could not live without Archie.

'I need to use the phone,' Archie said suddenly, interrupting the most wonderful silence. He seemed rather agitated. 'What now?' Amelia felt put out. They were together for the first time in months. Who on earth could he need to call now?

'I need to book a flight,' he said distractedly. 'Where are you going?' she asked, with evident disappointment. 'Peru,' he replied. 'I need to ask for your father's permission.' 'Permission for what?' Amelia was feeling confused. 'To marry you, of course.' He smiled indulgently, as if explaining a complicated point to a small child.

'You want to get married?' she asked incredulously. 'Oh, Amelia. I'm sorry. Of course, I should ask you properly.' With that, Archie got down on one knee, took Amelia's hand and, turning to face her, said: 'Amelia, darling, please make me the happiest man in the world by agreeing to become my wife.'

Amelia, with tears in her eyes, simply said, 'Yes, please.'

Cocktails for two...

Archie and Amelia, of course, wanted to celebrate their engagement. And what better way than with champagne cocktails? Here are a couple of Amelia's favourites. Not only do they taste delicious, but they are utterly uncomplicated to make...

Kir Royal

Simply divide the crème de cassis equally between two champagne flutes, then top with chilled champagne.

Ingredients

(Serves 2)

20ml crème de cassis

Champagne

Rose of the Ritz

This recipe was invented at the Ritz, Paris – surely the capital of romance.

Blend the raspberries, lemon juice, liqueur, Cognac and ice in a blender. Divide equally between two champagne flutes and top with chilled champagne.

Ingredients

(Serves 2)

20 fresh raspberries

Dash of lemon juice

50ml raspberry liqueur

50ml Cognac

Ice cubes

Champagne

From the heart...

True romance is not about grand gestures. It is the little things that mean a lot. Here is Amelia's list of nice things to do for your love:

✳ Make a compilation CD or tape of your songs and write on the cover where you first heard them or why they mean so much.

✳ Plant a tree in his name. It will last forever and, like love, will grow with each passing year.

✳ Make fortune cookies and put sweet messages in them.

✳ Make a memory box of your relationship and fill it with notes, photos, champagne corks, theatre tickets – whatever is special to the two of you.

✳ Create relationship rituals, whether it is ensuring you have brunch together every Sunday or making the first Monday of the month the day you go salsa dancing. These little traditions are the glue that holds you together.

✳ Don't be afraid to argue, but look after each other afterwards. Little notes left the morning after a row will make you both feel better.

Acknowledgements

As ever, there are so many people to thank. My brilliant friends who provide inspiration by being utterly gorgeous. Particularly, I'd like to thank William for his inimitable sense of style, Lucy for boosting my ego, Leigh for lengthy chats and Tristan for making me laugh and for endless technical support.

I'd also like to say a huge thank you to Anthony Topping for helping turn my idea into a book; to Lucy Truman for bringing Amelia to life so beautifully; to Sonya Nathoo for her gorgeous designs; to Annabel Morgan for being a brilliant editor; and Alison Starling for buying into Amelia so wholeheartedly.

And finally my delicious family – Lucie, Tatti, Jack and Toby – who make me giggle every day, and Tim, without whom I couldn't have done this. A huge talent and a warm heart is a rare combination.